DATE DUE

AUG. 2 ~ 1986		
OCT 7 1986		
APR 1 0 1987		
APR 27 1994		
201-6503		Printed in USA

Tricia Tusa

Chicken

Macmillan Publishing Company
New York

Collier Macmillan Publishers
London

© 1982 by Houghton Mifflin Company. Definition of
"chicken" reprinted by permission from the AMERICAN
HERITAGE DICTIONARY, SECOND COLLEGE EDITION.

Macmillan Publishing Company
866 Third Avenue, New York, N.Y. 10022
Collier Macmillan Canada, Inc.
Printed in the United States of America
10 9 8 7 6 5 4 3 2 1

The text of this book is set in 12 pt. Palatino.
The illustrations are preseparated, rendered in pen-and-ink,
and reproduced in three colors.

Library of Congress Cataloging in Publication Data
Tusa, Tricia.
Chicken.
Summary: A young chicken experiences an identity
crisis when he's called a chicken and finds that the
word means "timid and cowardly."
[1. Identity—Fiction.   2. Self-acceptance—Fiction.
3. Chickens—Fiction]   I. Title.
PZ7.T8825Ch   1986   [E]   85-10591
ISBN 0-02-789320-0

To the real Fran Moran, with dearest love

Fran Moran had driven to a nearby chicken farm to buy some extra-fresh eggs for breakfast.

As she placed them on her kitchen table, she saw one move.

Oh, dear, she thought, *this egg is about to hatch.*

By slowly rolling the egg between her hands, Fran gave it the warmth and motion it needed. She could feel the pecking and poking from inside. Within minutes, the egg cracked open and out swaggered a tiny chick.

"Goodness gracious me!" cried Fran with a big smile. Fran fed the chick warm water, milk, and oatmeal with an eye dropper. "Why, I'll call you Dooley—Dooley Fenton III—after my late uncle."

Dooley chirped with pleasure.

Fran continued to take care of Dooley, and they became close friends.
Dooley escorted Fran to all social events, adorning her festive hats.

And he was always willing to help with the chores.

As Dooley grew older, he began to wonder about himself. He saw that other winged creatures could fly, and he knew that he could not.

One day, inspired by a crow, he tried over and over again. He stood on the fence, spread his wings, tried to balance, jumped, flapped— and landed right on his head. "Oh, why can't I fly?" Dooley sighed.

"Because you are a chicken," said the crow. "Chickens can't fly."

"I am a what?" said Dooley.

"A chicken," repeated the crow. And before Dooley could question her further, she spread her wide, black wings and flew into the air..

Dooley went straight to the dictionary and looked up the new word.
Chicken...adj...Afraid; timid...To act in a cowardly manner;
lose one's nerve....

Without reading the rest of the definition, Dooley slammed the book shut and sat there, stunned. "Oh, dear, is this the reason I can't fly? Am I a coward? No! It can't be!"

Dooley ran outside to Alpo, the pet dog. "Alpo, Alpo, what am I?" he asked.

Alpo lifted her head slowly and said in her southern drawl, "Now, suga', you're a chicken, you know that."

Dooley squawked and fluttered on down the road.

He headed toward the meadow and approached the cow. "What do *you* think I am?" he asked.

"I don't *think*. I know for a fact that you are a chicken. Now stop bothering me. I am in the middle of my morning snack." The cow continued munching the grass.

Dooley returned to the house with his head low. Coming upon a chubby earthworm, he said softly, "Excuse me. From your point of view, who am I?"

"Well, since I don't know you personally, all I can say for certain is that you are a chicken."

Dooley dragged his tail all the way back to his bed, where he lay for hours, thinking. "So, in the eyes of the world, I am a chicken." Dooley whimpered quietly.

Fran could not understand it. A definite change had come over her precious Dooley. And she could see that he did not want to talk about it. He seemed embarrassed.

Dooley had begun to believe he was a coward. Suddenly, he was afraid to be alone.

He became terrified of the rain and would hide until the sun came out.

But the sunlight sent him scurrying for shade.

He began to tremble at the sight of dust and carried a duster every-
where.

Dooley became timid with Fran's friends. He perspired heavily
around other animals and fainted on hearing loud noises.

Even the television scared him.

Then, one bright spring Sunday, Fran decided to attend the annual Azalea Trail Festival. That meant going from house to house to see the lovely azaleas blooming in the gardens all over town. Of course, Dooley did not want to be in a crowd, but he was more afraid of staying home alone.

As the tour was about to begin, the guide approached Fran. Dooley cowered in her bonnet. "Madam," said the tour guide, "I have ordered a wheelchair for your convenience. We have a long distance to cover and don't want to be slowed down by someone your age."

"Why, you young whippersnapper—" Fran began. But before she could finish, Dooley leaped from his hiding place.

"How dare you!" he squawked. "Ms. Moran could walk through these gardens twice and a third time backward before you could get halfway through!"

At that, the crowd chuckled and cheered. Dooley blushed—but he did not retreat behind Fran's hat brim, for he felt like his old self again.

After returning home from the outing, Fran and Dooley set their tea out on the terrace. "Dooley," Fran asked gently, "where are your sunglasses?"

"I don't need them anymore, Fran. I know who I am. I don't care what anyone else thinks. I'm no chicken!"

"But, Dooley, you *are* a ... Dooley, why don't you want to be a chicken?"

"Because a chicken is a coward!" said Dooley.

"Where did you learn that nonsense?"

"When I asked who I was, everyone said I was a chicken. So I looked it up in the dictionary."

"Poor Dooley," said Fran. And she scooped him under one arm. Under the other she tucked the dictionary. Then off she drove to the chicken farm.

"Dear, dear Dooley, you are indeed a chicken. And these are other chickens. This is where you came from."

Fran opened the dictionary. "I'm afraid you overlooked something," she said. She then read, "*Chicken...noun...The common domestic fowl....* Dooley, you are not chicken. You are *a* chicken—and a very special friend."

And so Fran Moran and Dooley Fenton III were able to resume their happy life together—now that Dooley had learned to see himself through his own eyes and no one else's.